Unforgiving Scream

When Leslie Cries, Volume 3

Amy Richie

Published by Amy Richie, 2018.

UNFORGIVING SCREAM

First edition. November 28, 2018.

Copyright © 2018 Amy Richie.

ISBN: 979-8227996015

Written by Amy Richie.

Unforgiving Scream
Book Three

Dr. Matthews cleared his throat quietly and continued to stare at me. Leslie refused to talk to him and she didn't want me to talk to him either; as a result, the past several sessions had ended up with him just staring a lot and clearing his throat. As Leslie said, he couldn't force us to talk.

"I know things have been difficult for you, Mellie," he finally broke the silence when there were only a few minutes left of the session, "but you can't keep letting Leslie speak for you."

Without replying, I turned my head so I could see outside. The clouds were gathering up for a storm. I used to love when it stormed at home; I loved the smell of the rain on the wind and watching the fat drops of water hit the ground.

"If she keeps taking over, you might get lost forever."

Maybe that was for the best.

"Times up," Leslie announced.

~

"Listen to this line right here," Leslie stabbed at the single sheet of paper with one finger.

"We've already read it," I grumbled. "Like twenty times."

"It isn't often that we hear from your mother," Leslie smiled a large fake smile. "I think it's important to listen to every word she says."

"We have," I reminded her again. "It's really not a very good letter." Mom only wrote once every few weeks and none of her letters were encouraging. Mostly they were just lists of things she had done, details of her small apartment, or a play by play of her recent dates.

"She cut her hair," Leslie scoffed.

"Not exactly headline news." I pulled gently at the jagged strands of my own hair that had finally grown out enough to touch my shirt collar. "People cut their hair all the time."

Leslie's eyes widened almost comically. "Not your prissy mother."

Shrugging, I turned away from the letter so I could stare out the barred window in the day room. I wasn't all that interested in what my prissy mother had to say. That didn't stop Leslie from reading it over and over again, dissecting each line.

"And this right here," she poked the paper again, "you think she'll really come to visit?"

"She always says that," I reminded her dully. At the end of every one of her letters, she promised that she would ask Dr. Matthews if she could come for a visit. I hadn't seen her in a very long time.

"She better not." Her top lip curled up in a snarl. "I don't want to see that bitch."

She didn't want to see us either; Leslie had nothing to worry about.

"Do you think your mom is getting any action from this new boyfriend of hers?"

Suddenly too tired to hold myself upright, I slumped forward until my cheek could rest on the table in front of me.

Why did she care so much about what was in that letter? It didn't mean anything.

"Hey," Skinny Carrie's voice cut across the room. "You can't sleep in here," she informed me, kicking the legs of my chair. "Wake up."

"Get away," Leslie warned in a low growl.

"No sleeping in the day room," she screeched again.

"Mind your own business," Leslie suggested in a way that made it clear it wasn't optional.

Carrie kicked the chair again. "I'll tell the nurse," she sang out.

Everything that happened next, happened very quickly. Before I'd even raised my head all the way off the table – it was over.

Enraged, Leslie had flew up from the table and pulled a fork from the waist band of her pants. In a flash, she heaved it into Carrie's thigh.

"I told you to shut up," Leslie panted triumphantly.

As Carrie's screams swelled dynamically, my mouth fell open in shock. Where did Leslie get a fork? How had she kept it hidden from the nurses and guard?

"I'm bleeding," Carrie screeched, "that crazy bitch stabbed me."

Leslie laughed loudly. "You deserved it," she sneered. "If you don't leave me alone, I'll stab you again."

The nurses swarmed around us, trying to figure out what had happened and why Carrie was bleeding. "Where did this fork come from?" the nurse gasped.

"From Mellie," Carrie wailed. "That bitch stabbed me."

The nurse turned wide eyes to me. "How did you...?"

"It wasn't me," I shook my head quickly. "I didn't do anything."

"Everyone saw you," Carrie screamed.

"It was... it was Leslie."

"Leslie?" Carrie scoffed. "How convenient."

"Get her to the hole," the nurse barked out.

I didn't bother wasting my breath to argue. Of course, Leslie wore my face, so whatever she did was my fault. Dr. Matthews had warned me that she would get out of control. "Whatever," I grumbled under my breath.

"And check her for any more weapons!"

"She's not even hurt," Leslie yelled. "She's fine."

Carrie's face contorted with pain as she pulled the fork from her leg by herself. Bright red blood blossomed out on her gray pants.

"Hospital wing," the nurse grunted. "And get Mellie out of here."

"Doesn't matter to me," Leslie shrugged wildly. "At least it's quiet back there."

~

"Looks like we're back again," Leslie declared loudly, pacing the small space. "This cozy little room is starting to feel just like home."

"Might as well sit down," I offered dully, pointing to the spot next to me on the soft floor.

"I'd rather stand," she huffed.

Shrugging, I leaned back until my head rested on the wall behind me. Leslie was right about one thing, I was starting to get used to being back in solitary.

Leslie always got me in trouble.

"I'm going to demand that they let us out," Leslie decided angrily.

"That's never worked before."

"You are so weak." Leslie glared at me.

A soft knock on the door saved me from any more of her anger. "Hey," Nurse Kaydee stuck her head in the room and smiled almost timidly. Her lips shook at the corners.

"What do you want?" Leslie snarled, apparently happy to have someone else to vent herself upon.

Nurse Kaydee's smile disappeared instantly and completely. "I brought lunch," she announced coldly.

"Not hungry."

Ignoring her, Nurse Kaydee came the rest of the way inside with a tray of food in her hands. "Chicken salad today," she deadpanned. "Mellie likes chicken salad."

Despite her dislike for Nurse Kaydee, Leslie smiled and let her set the tray down in front of me. "Must be her lucky day," she mocked.

"I want to talk to her."

"No." Leslie straightened her mouth and narrowed her eyes. She had already said I wasn't allowed to talk to Nurse Kaydee and I was too tired to fight the issue. Besides, it wasn't like I had anything to say to her anyways. Dr. Matthews and his team of nurses only wanted to stare at me these days – no thanks.

"I just want to see if she's ok."

"She's fine," Leslie glided next to me so she could put her hand on my shoulder. "She has me."

"Ask her if she wants to talk to me," Nurse Kaydee snapped.

"I'm not..."

"I will," I cut Leslie off. "I'll talk to Nurse Kaydee."

"We talked about this," she hissed. "It's not good for you to talk to them."

"I want to." I turned my face so I could see Leslie. "It's fine."

Despite the tightening of her lips, she nodded and faded to the dark corner of the room.

"You wanted to see if I was ok?" I turned dull eyes to Nurse Kaydee.

"Mellie?"

"Yeah." I meant to smile but I wasn't sure if my lips were moving in the right direction or not.

"I brought you lunch."

"Chicken salad." I was right there when she told Leslie, didn't she know that?

"Dr. Matthews has been worried about you," she gushed, taking a few steps towards me. "We all have."

"Why?"

"Because..." I watched her tongue shoot out to run across her top lip. Was she nervous? "Because we don't get to talk to you very much these days. We just need to be sure you're still ok."

"I guess you already know I'm not – other wise you wouldn't be worried." I took a small bite of the pile of mushy meat that they called chicken salad. "My mom used to make really good chicken salad," I suddenly remembered.

"Mellie," she took a deep breath, "how are you feeling?"

"I'm scared," I whispered.

"Scared of what? Are you scared of Leslie?"

"No. I'm scared of myself."

"That's enough," Leslie burst from the shadows. "Leave her alone to eat."

"We're still talking," Nurse Kaydee tried to insist.

"No, you're not." Everyone in that tiny room knew Leslie was right.

~

"I see that you spent another night in solitary," Dr. Matthews observed, his eyes scanning the pages in front of him.

"Did your precious nurses write all that down for you?" Leslie sneered, making her top lip flip up.

"I've read the reports," he replied calmly.

"Good job." She flung herself back on the couch.

"Nurse Kaydee says that you talked for yourself, Mellie," he continued slowly.

The sound of my name made me jump slightly. Of course I could speak for myself, why did he sound so surprised? I squirmed uncomfortably on my seat.

"Ugh," Leslie made a low sound in her throat. "I shouldn't have let Mellie talk to that woman."

"Why not?" Dr. Matthews asked for me.

"Of course she would make a big deal out of it."

"I think she's just concerned."

"Mellie is safe, I'm keeping her safe."

Dr. Matthews worked his jaw in a rigid motion but didn't reply. "Your mother wants to come visit, Mellie."

"What?" I choked, shock making me speak to him for the first time in weeks.

"She called this morning and set up a visitation."

"No way."

"We've decided on tomorrow afternoon," he continued, shaking his head as if I were agreeing to it.

"I don't want to see my mother."

Dr. Matthews took a deep breath and blew it out slowly. "She's been asking to see you for a few months now," he reminded me.

"You said I don't have to see her."

"I think the reminder of the person you were before would be a good idea."

"I'm..." I ran my tongue over my top lip. How could I explain to calm Dr. Matthews that I wasn't the same person anymore? I didn't need to be reminded of that girl because that girl wasn't real anymore. To see me now would only upset my mom. "I don't want to see her," I finished lamely.

"It's been decided. The nurse will bring you when it's time."

~

"Why don't you try playing cards with Janice?" Nurse Kaydee suggested with a small grin. She pointed out the empty seat at Janice's table.

"We're sitting there," Leslie steered me to an empty seat without a backwards glance to Nurse Kaydee. "Why does she always want you to play cards?"

"She probably just doesn't want me to sit here alone."

"You're not alone."

"They don't count you."

"Whatever," Leslie scoffed. "Cards are boring and Janice cheats."

"I don't want to play."

"Of course you don't." Leslie glared between Janice and Nurse Kaydee, letting her eyebrows knit together and lips purse. My thoughts soon began to wander away from her and the day room.

"Watch this hand very closely," Beth wriggled her eyebrows and grinned stupidly.

"Magic tricks are stupid." Still, I kept my eyes on her hand - watching for the moment when the string would disappear.

"This one is good."

"Where did you learn it?"

"My teacher." She tried to keep her voice low but the giggle ruined the effect. "Now watch this hand."

Rolling my eyes for all I was worth, I refocused on her closed hand. Suddenly, with her other hand, she jabbed her finger into my cheek.

"Gotcha," she squealed, laughing full out.

"But..." I pried open her closed hand. A small piece of string was balled up on her palm. "The string is still here."

"Oh my gosh, Mellie," her laughter turned to a sigh. "Did you have any friends at all?"

"Yes."

Beth tugged lightly at my protruding bottom lip. "You're so silly."

"No, I'm not."

"And pretty."

A flame started to burn in my stomach.
"And you smell good."
The flame traveled up my neck.
"And I love the way you pout."
"I don't pout." Heat popped out of my cheeks.
"You do."
"I don't."
"But it's so cute."

"Why are you smiling like that?" Leslie demanded, pulling my thoughts back to the dreary reality of the day room.

"What?"

"You're smiling," she accused. "What are you thinking about?"

"Nothing."

"Beth."

Why did she even bother asking? It wasn't like I could hide anything from her anyways. "So?"

"You shouldn't be thinking about that girl."

So she was *that girl* now? "Why not?" I liked thinking about Beth.

"You need to be thinking of how we're going to get out of your visit with mommy tomorrow."

"There's no way out of that." Leslie knew that too.

"We could throw a fit and get put into solitary," she suggested, pressing her finger into her chin.

"I don't want to."

"It doesn't really matter what you want."

When did that happen?

~

"It's been a while," mom said from across the table. Her lips turned up into a half smile that stopped before it ever reached her eyes.

"Mmmm," I grunted, not sure what I was expected to say. I wasn't even sure how long it had been since I saw her. She seemed different. Dark puffy circles made her eyes look smaller and there were more lines at the corners of her mouth than before. Did that mean she was smiling more? I racked my brain for forgotten news about a boyfriend she might have had.

"How have you been?"

I shrugged, then ran my tongue across my bottom lip. She probably wanted me to talk. "The same as before."

"The same as what?" There was a familiar bite in her voice. "Before Leslie?"

Shifting uncomfortably in my chair, I glanced quickly at Leslie. "No, not quite before that."

"At least you're looking better than last year after that one girl killed herself."

I flinched from her cruel words. "Yeah."

"I still can't believe they let something like that happen here. You'd think they would watch you girls better than that." She clicked her tongue loudly against the roof of her mouth.

"When are you leaving?" Leslie snapped angrily.

"Don't be so rude, I just got here. Didn't you miss me?"

"Did you miss me?" I already knew she didn't but I wondered how she would reply. Especially with Dr. Matthews sitting at the table with us, writing away in his stupid notebook.

"What?"

"I asked if you missed me."

"I heard what you asked."

"Then?"

"What kind of a question is that?" She looked to Dr. Matthews but he remained stoic. "Why would I come all the way here if I didn't miss you?"

"Sense of duty?"

"You're not a child anymore, Mellie. I came because I wanted to, not because I have to."

The sounds of Dr. Matthews scribbling filled the stale air.

"I can't really stay long though."

"Hot date?"

"Twenty minute visitations." She pursed her lips tight.

"Oh." Surely it had already been about that long. Why did she even come all this way for a short, awkward visit?

"Your father is getting remarried," she blurted after another long pause.

"What?"

"He found some slut on the internet."

"Dad?"

"Yep," she nodded forcefully, making her short hair flop on her forehead. "Apparently he joined a dating site and found someone willing to marry him."

"That's...weird."

"I know." Mom chuckled lightly.

~

"I don't know why she has to come here," Leslie sulked. She sat in her usual place on the floor, across from my bed.

"She probably just hopes I'm better," I murmured sleepily.

"Better?"

"You know what I mean...normal."

"You're never going to be normal, Mellie."

"I know." I had spent years of my life in a mental hospital; normal wasn't in the cards for me. Not even the crazy cards that Janice played. "But she still hopes I will be some day."

"I'm not going to let her talk to you like that next time she comes."

"She wasn't that bad." For mom, she was actually kind of nice.

"You sleep." Her voice was becoming more muffled. "I'll take care of everything."

"You always do," I replied sleepily.

~

A small beam of light flashed across my pupils, making me squint. "Put the fork down," a sharp voice ordered.

"What?"

"I'm not going to ask you again," the voice got louder. "Put it down before you hurt someone."

"What fork?" I blinked rapidly, trying to see past the small beam of light. "Where am I?"

The room around me was completely dark. I had just laid down to sleep so why was I standing up now? This place didn't even look like my room.

"Drop the fork that's in your hand."

It was only after he said it did I realize that my hand was clutched around the cool metal of a fork. "This isn't mine." Was I in the cafeteria? I tried to make out the dark shapes of the tables.

"Drop it."

Obediently, I opened my fingers to let the fork clatter to the floor. The sound echoed in the empty room. "I don't understand."

"Leslie?" Nurse Kaydee stepped forward into the small pool of light. "Why did you come back here?"

"Nurse Kaydee," I lunged forward, eager to grasp onto anything that made sense.

"Stay where you are," she held her hand out between us. "Why are you back here?"

"I have no idea." I looked wildly around us, not recognizing anything except her. "I was sleeping."

"Leslie..."

"She's not here." Eyes wide, I shook my head back and forth.

"Melody?"

"W...why are you saying my name like that?" She never called me Melody. And why did she sound so scared?

"Is that you?" There was a tremor in her voice that I didn't like.

"Of course."

~

"State your name." There was a stiffness in Dr. Matthews' posture and his face looked more lined than usual.

Heaving a huge sigh, I rolled my eyes. "I don't know why everyone is being so weird," I complained. "You already know my name."

"Just..." He took a deep breath of his own, "just state your name for me."

"Melody Parker."

"Not Leslie?"

"Leslie isn't here," I told him – again. "I haven't seen her since I went to sleep last night."

Dr. Matthews pulled his hand roughly down his lined face.

"Are you alright, Dr. Matthews?" He didn't look alright.

"What happened?"

"Last night?"

He nodded slowly. "Why were you back in that hallway?"

"I don't remember." My eyebrows puckered with the strain of trying to find the memory. How could I just black out like that and not even remember walking to an entirely different room?

"What's the last thing you do remember?"

"I was talking to Leslie in my room and then I fell asleep." We had already talked about this too.

Dr. Matthews jumped up suddenly and pulled his chair closer to the couch I was sitting on. "Do you remember anything else?" His words were intense, scary intense.

"Why are you sitting so close to me?"

"What did you two talk about?"

"Ummm..." It was hard to remember anything at all with him staring at me like that. "Leslie was mad."

"Why?" he prompted hastily, moving forward more in his chair to put himself even closer to me.

"She was mad because...." Why was she mad? Leslie was always mad about something. "It was because of mom's visit," I recalled. "She didn't want her to come here." It wasn't enough of a surprise to warrant Dr. Matthews' sharp intake of breath. "Leslie has never liked mom," I explained breathlessly. "She's always in a bad mood when she sees her."

"Your mother hasn't been in to visit you in a long time, Mellie." His eyes still hadn't gone to their normal size, which was probably why my lungs were starting to push the air out faster.

"She was here yesterday."

"No, she wasn't."

It wouldn't be the first time I had lost track of a few days. Sometimes whole weeks would go by and it seemed like a few days to me; Beth said it was the pills that made me lose time. Dr. Matthews blamed Leslie. It wasn't the first time – so why was he looking at me like that and why was my heart suddenly racing inside my chest?

"How long?"

"The last time your mother visited here was," he cleared his throat lightly, "a little over six years ago."

The world momentarily blurred out of focus. "That's ridiculous," I heard myself mumble.

"We knew Leslie was taking over completely but there wasn't anything we could do about it without your help." Despite the shaking in the room, Dr. Matthews kept talking as if I could hear him. "...a new drug trial..."

"What?"

"We started a new drug last month, it's a trial."

"Did it kill her?"

"I..."

"She's not here."

"It's impossible to know if she's gone for good. It's likely we'll have to adjust the meds as we go along. At least you're awake now. We can begin..." Dr. Matthews' voice wavered again with the room.

Six years? Mom had come to visit me six years ago? How? Did Leslie just keep me sleeping that whole time? But then... "Did Leslie do anything bad while I was...sleeping?"

Dr. Matthews' lips snapped closed.

"So yes?"

"I think we need to focus on moving forward," he suggested stiffly.

So...*really* bad.

~

My lips made a circle as I pushed the air out forcefully. I could hear the air moving back through my nose and down to my lungs again. I pushed it back out again.

"I don't think I'm going to go to sleep tonight," I informed Nurse Kaydee.

Her fingers shook when she straightened my bed cover for the third time. "Lack of sleep will only make it easier for her to take over again," she said softly, almost a whisper. She was probably afraid Leslie would hear her.

"Was she mean to you?" The words tumbled from my lips in the same fearful whisper.

"It wasn't you."

"She's a part of me though." Leslie was a part of me and she wore my face.

"Everyone," she took a deep breath and when she spoke again, the tremble was gone from her voice, "every single one of us has a Leslie that lives deep inside of us. Yours just escaped."

"Why though?" I wrapped my arms tightly around my waist. "Is it because I'm not strong enough to control her?"

"Something terrible happened to you, Mellie. There's not many people who would be strong enough to handle that."

Dr. Matthews had explained it to me, many times. I had created Leslie to deal with what Ethan had done to me. Through Leslie, I became strong enough.

"Do you think..." I ran my tongue over my dry lips, "do you think I'll be able to stop her?"

"Yes."

I looked up at her, surprised by the force of the word. "Really?"

"I know you are." She sucked in her lips. "But you need to be strong, so you need to sleep and eat and take your medicine. Don't let her talk you into being weak."

"Will she be here when I wake up?"

"I don't know."

Swallowing hard, I nodded.

"The pills are working though, we'll help you get through this."

~

Mellie!

My eyes, which had been hard to close in the first place, popped back open. Raspy breaths echoed in my ears. At first glance, I didn't see her sitting in the corner. It was only after my second sweep did I see her.

"Leslie."

Her lips turned up into a chilling smile. "It's been a while," she said in a low voice.

"So I've heard," I whispered back.

"Did you have a nice sleep?"

She was definitely Leslie, but the time had drastically changed my once upon a time protector. Her beautiful face was gaunt with shadows and sneers, bags puffed out her eyes until they seemed sunken into her face, her hair hung in clumps down past her neck.

"What happened to you?" I shot out, making her sneer harder.

"It's been a lot of work," she sighed.

"What has?" I felt my eyebrows pucker.

"Keeping you asleep."

My heart stuttered and then sped up to double time. "Why didn't you just wake me up then?"

"Well," she tilted her face as if she were deep in thought, "at first I just wanted you to be safe."

"What do you mean at first? What about now?"

"Now," she turned to look directly at me, "I like being you. I don't think there's room enough for both of us in this world."

"You can't...you can't just make me leave. That's not..."

"It's not my fault you're weak," Leslie shrugged one shoulder. "Everyone was better off without you."

"I'm not weak." Even my declaration was weak though.

"Hmm," she grunted a small laugh. "We'll see, won't we?"

~

"So," a girl with short blonde hair plopped down on the empty chair at my table, "have you decided?"

"What?" I looked up at her, eyes wide.

"Have you decided?" she repeated, slower – as if that would help me understand what I was supposed to be deciding.

"Umm," I closed and opened my mouth several times, "I don't know."

"What's wrong with you?" She slammed her hand on the table, making me jump.

Turning my body as much as possible, I dipped my head low to block out the view of the girl. My hair had grown out while I was sleeping, long enough to fall into my face. "Go away," I grunted, failing to put the proper anger into my words.

"Go away?" the girl laughed loudly. "I don't know what you're trying to pull but it's not going to work."

"I don't know who you are," I peeked out at her, "so just leave me alone."

Without warning, she lunged across the table and grabbed a fistful of my hair. "You know who I am," she growled.

"Let go of me!" Tears sprang to my eyes.

"Nadia, let go," Nurse Kaydee hurried across the room. "Right now."

"She's pretending not to know me," the girl called Nadia yelled back, but her grip did loosen on my hair.

"Mellie has had a very hard couple of days," Nurse Kaydee explained.

"She said never to call her Mellie." Nadia released my head with a rough shove.

"Regardless of her name," another nurse bustled over to the scene, "pulling hair is not acceptable behavior in the day room." Her nostrils flared. "Back to your room, Nadia."

My gaze swung over to Nurse Kaydee, her eyes were sympathetic. Why did this girl hate me? Or better yet, what had Leslie done to her?

~

The hand that held my spoon shook slightly as I attempted to swirl spaghetti noodles around it. Nurse Kaydee had assured me that I would get my fork privileges back after I proved I could be trusted. For now I just had to do the best I could with a spoon.

Two tables away, Nadia glared at me with eyes so narrowed they barely looked open. Her skin was too pale to be healthy and she had the customary dark circles under her eyes. She was probably once very pretty, I decided. One bad hair cut and who knew how many sleepless nights had obviously changed her. Maybe she should try smiling.

"Why does your face look like that?" Leslie hissed, pulling her lips back from her teeth in a half growl.

"Look like what?" Nadia almost whimpered, pulling her knees closer to her chest.

"Like someone kicked you."

"Leave me alone."

"I'm afraid I can't." Without any warning, Leslie pulled back her leg and kicked Nadia's hands – hard enough to make her drop them away from her knees and sprawl forward.

I sucked in a shallow breath. Hopefully, that hadn't really happened.

Nadia took an aggressive bite of her bread and chewed it slowly, keeping her eyes on me the entire time.

"Ok," I whispered. Evidently it had really happened. No wonder she hated me.

~

Leslie was sitting in the middle of my bed when I returned from supper. Following Dr. Matthews' advice, I immediately averted my gaze and tried to go about my business as if she wasn't there at all. I flipped on the water in my tiny sink and counted to thirty before dipping my toothpaste under the stream.

"You don't need to do that," Leslie called from behind me. "There's nothing in the water, Beth was wrong."

Weird how the sound of Beth's name on Leslie's tongue made the hairs on the back of my neck stick up.

"You know what I think is funny?" she continued to taunt despite my silence. "That you still do that even though she's been dead for like seven years."

"Hilarious," I grunted. Thankfully, my eyes were beginning to feel heavy from the sleeping pill the nurse gave me. I wouldn't have to hear her for much longer.

"You're going to regret trying to push me out."

"I doubt it."

"You're not strong enough without me."

When I turned to argue that I was, Leslie was already gone.

~

"They told me you're crazy." Nadia slid onto the seat in front of me and slammed her full tray of food down.

"Everyone here is crazy," I reminded her, careful not to look up from my own lunch.

"Yeah, but you're a special kind of crazy."

There were plenty of empty tables in the cafeteria, why did she have to sit with me? "What do you want?"

"What's your name?"

My teeth paused in their chewing and I swung my gaze up to her. "What?"

"Your name," she snapped, "what is it?"

"Melody."

Her eyes widened, then narrowed again. "Janice told me to ask you."

"Why?"

Nadia shrugged. "Guess she knew you were a liar."

"I'm not a liar." My forehead puckered. "Why can't you sit somewhere else?"

"Your name is Melody?" It was clear by her scowl that she didn't believe me.

"People call me Mellie."

"I've only ever heard people call you Leslie."

I shifted my eyes back down to my food as the blood drained from my face. "I'm not Leslie," was all I could think of to say.

"You were just a few days ago."

"No, I wasn't." My throat burned with the accusation. "She must have been...mean to you."

Nadia laughed a bark-like sound. "Mean doesn't begin to cover it." Her face twisted up into a snarl. "And I don't believe you for one second."

"Believe me about Leslie?"

"You are Leslie and you didn't just forget that."

"Maybe you should change seats," I suggested again.

"We're not allowed to switch seats." She picked up a carrot stick and bit it in half, all the while watching me.

"There's no assigned seats."

"True," she drawled. "But you can't move after you sit down."

"I'm..." I glanced around the room, "I'm sure you can."

"They changed the rule years ago." Her eyes narrowed as she continued to dramatically chew her carrot stick.

My cheeks puffed out with a mouth full of air. What else had changed while I was sleeping?

~

"Hello there," the woman sitting across from me smiled so wide, I was afraid her face was going to break.

"Umm...hi," I replied awkwardly. "I'm not really sure who you are."

"We've been meeting together for almost three years." Her smile didn't even twitch.

"Oh." That didn't really help.

"Leslie...," she faltered through her smile, "seems to like me better than Dr. Matthews."

"She hates Dr. Matthews."

The woman nodded. "We just thought it would be nice for her to have someone to talk to."

"What do you guys talk about?" My heart was hammering hard against my chest; this whole thing didn't feel real.

"Leslie is very angry, we've been trying to work through that."

I traced the light swirling designs on the top of my slipper with one finger that I couldn't keep still. "Dr. Matthews said if we treat her like she's real, she'll never go away."

Her smile faltered for the first time. "We have slightly different opinions on treatment."

If the two doctors couldn't even agree on how to get rid of Leslie, was there any hope for me? "I want her to go away for good."

"Well then, at least we can all agree on the most important thing," she smiled again.

"So what do we do now?"

"The two of us can talk if you'd like."

How could we talk if she didn't even have a notebook in her lap? "I like Dr. Matthews."

"That's good," she nodded encouragingly.

"Are you even a doctor?"

"Leslie asked me the same question." She almost laughed, as if that were a funny thing – me and Leslie being the same.

"What did you tell her?" I pulled my arms tight over my chest.

"My name is Dr. Simmons but you can call me Martha."

"Why would I call you Martha?" We weren't friends.

Dr. Simmons pressed her lips tight together, then nodded. "What do you want me to call you?"

"My name." My tongue glided over my top lip. "It's Melody."

~

"Mellie?"

"Yeah?" I shook my head quickly and refocused on Nurse Kaydee. She held a small white cup out to me. *Don't take the pills here. That's how they control us.* But Beth wasn't here anymore, she didn't see how bad Leslie had gotten. I needed their pills.

"Med pass," Nurse Kaydee shook the cup at me.

"Thanks," I mumbled, throwing the pills into my mouth with a sip of water to chase them down my throat.

"Have you seen Leslie today?"

My eyes shifted automatically to the window seat where Leslie usually sat. She wasn't there now, but she had been when I first walked in. "Just for a second," I admitted in a hoarse whisper. I hated to see that pucker between Nurse Kaydee's eyes, the pucker that meant something was wrong. What if the pills stopped working? My heart sped up.

"Did she talk to you?"

"No."

She smiled gently. "We're having music in a little bit. That should be nice."

"Music?"

"Dottie's coming to sing today."

Swallowing past my objections, I nodded.

"I don't know why we have to listen to that old bat," Carrie complained loudly. "Can't you guys get us someone who can actually sing?"

She got no sympathy from the nurses, although she did get a few cat calls from the girls who apparently agreed with her sentiments. My lips turned up in the corners.

"So, who are you today?" Nadia sat down across from me, nostrils flared and unsmiling lips.

"Melody."

She leaned far across the table. "I don't like your name."

"Umm..."

"Or your face."

"Then why are you sitting here?" If she hated me so much, why was she always seeking me out?

"Because..." She leaned back with a huff, crossing her arms over her chest. "I'm trying to figure you out."

"It's best if you don't."

"Why? Are you scared of me?" She laughed lightly, but didn't relax her arms.

"Leslie wasn't nice to you." Her sneer froze. "And I have no idea when she'll be back. I can't control her yet." It didn't escape my comfort level to be talking about Leslie so freely, as if she were a separate person. I knew she was me – and yet...she wasn't me at the same time. If I couldn't figure me out, Nadia definitely shouldn't try.

"Did you just make her up?"

"What?"

"Leslie," she clarified, "did you just make her up so you could be pissed at people without your halo slipping?"

"I don't..." I shook my head quickly, "I don't know why she came." There was no way I was telling this girl about Ethan Sturgis.

"I heard you killed someone."

"We all killed someone."

Nadia sucked in a breath through her teeth that came across as a hiss. "I don't trust you, *Melody*."

"I didn't ask you to trust me," I reminded her. "And I didn't ask you to sit with me." Seeing that she wasn't going to move, I got up from my seat and squished myself on the already full couch.

"Find somewhere else to sit, Mellie," Carrie screeched. "Or Leslie if that's who you want to be today."

"Shut up, Carrie," I scowled. "You're skinny enough to share this cushion with me."

"Dr. Matthews said you're not allowed to make fun of my weight," she bellowed into my face.

"Shut up," I said again, much calmer than her.

"I like you better as Leslie," she declared. "She would have never been run off the table by Nadia."

"Are you going to shut up?" Nadia yelled from her place at the table.

"Whatever," Carrie threw herself back against the couch in a huff.

Across the room, I caught Nadia's eye. She was staring openly at me, her expression unguarded and curious. I hurried to look away.

~

"Ladies," Dottie gushed from the front of the room.

"She's so weird," Carrie sneered from the seat in front of me. "She comes in here all the time and tells us how much she loves us and how beautiful we are."

"There you go, Mellie," Janice grinned, "she seems like your type."

"You're disgusting," I kicked the back of her chair.

Carrie laughed loudly, the sound coming out like a hiccup. "You want me to ask her out for you, Mellie? You guys could grab a bite to eat in the cafeteria." She bent low to her knees, laughing and clutching at her sides.

"Tomorrow is pizza day," Janice chimed in, winking ludicrously.

"I'm so happy you're all here," Dottie continued to simper.

"I don't know why she's so happy we're here," came a dry voice from next to me. Nadia had sidled in while I was rolling my eyes at Janice and Carrie.

"What are you, some kind of stalker?" I growled. "Stop following me around."

Nadia didn't blink. "We all have to come in here to listen to the music."

"There's other chairs."

"I wanted this one."

"Why?"

Nadia turned to face the front of the room. "They don't even question that you changed into a new person over night."

Resigned, I settled back into my own seat. "We live in a loony bin," I shrugged. "There's a lot of things you don't question here."

"I've been here for almost six months already." Her gaze stayed fixed, straight ahead.

"I've been here longer than that." I couldn't even remember now exactly how long I'd been there, but it was longer than six months.

"You've hated me from the moment you saw me." She sucked in her bottom lip but kept staring forward. "Why?"

"I...I haven't been myself lately."

"What did I ever do to you?"

"Probably nothing," I sighed. Leslie didn't always need a reason to hate someone.

~

"Do you need something to help you sleep tonight?" Nurse Kaydee asked, shaking the small white bottle with no label in my direction.

"I don't know." I sat on the edge of my bed with my hands tucked under my legs, trying not to let her see how much they were shaking.

"Is Leslie here?"

"No." My lips snapped shut before I could give away too much information. *Just answer the question they ask.*

She took a short breath through her nose and narrowed her eyes as she peered down at me. "Here." She shook two pills out into my outstretched hand. "I'll feel better if I know you're in here sleeping and not talking to Leslie."

As soon as she left the room, the lights went out. It would have been nice to sleep with the lights on, but that was against the rules and I knew better than to ask. I had never been afraid of the dark before, until Leslie pointed out the things that could be hiding there.

"Hey," a familiar voice called out softly.

Without turning to look at her, I whispered, "You're not supposed to be in here."

"Says who?" Leslie snarled. "Dr. Matthews doesn't get to tell me what to do anymore."

"They gave me medicine to make you disappear." My voice sounded braver than I felt.

"And yet, here I am."

I chewed nervously on the side of my thumb. "Can I ask you something?"

"Sure." I heard the humor in her tone.

"What did you do to Nadia?"

"I hate that bitch."

"Why?"

"She's ugly."

"That's not true."

"You think she's pretty?"

"I mean," I cleared my throat softly, "that isn't why you don't like her."

"No."

I was surprised how readily she admitted to it. "Then why?"

"She knew Ethan."

My mouth, that had been working on a loose piece of skin, froze. "What?" I mumbled.

"I remember seeing her at a few of those house parties. She talked to him, she knew him."

"Are you sure?"

"Positive."

Without thinking about it, I rolled over to my side so I could see her. "That's crazy."

"Says the girl locked in a loony bin."

Nadia knew Ethan? Were they close? Did she know that I had... did she know what had happened that summer? My mind was still whirling when the sleeping pills took over.

"You better not even think of being friends with her," Leslie snarled out, right before my eyelids became too heavy to hold open.

~

"I saw her last night," I muttered, keeping my eyes on my twisted fingers.

"Where at?" Dr. Matthews stiffened slightly, but I noticed.

"She was in my room."

"Did you talk to her?"

"A little."

"Hmmm." His pen glided across the paper.

"Does that mean the medicine isn't working anymore?" Fear tried to nestle into my chest, making it hard to get a full breath.

"She didn't take over," he said slowly. "You remember the incident."

"So...?"

"So, that means it's still working like it should."

"But why do I still see her?" My throat burned with the tears that were filling my eyes.

"It's going to take time," he said gently. "Time for you to learn how to deal with Leslie."

"Do you think I'll ever get to leave here and have a real life?"

"Is that what you want?"

I wasn't sure what a real life meant, really; but I did know that I didn't want to stay in a prison my whole life. "Yeah, I think so."

"Then that's what you'll get." He smiled until his eyes crinkled at the corners.

I didn't smile back.

~

"Mellie or Leslie?" Carrie grinned down at me, showing her uneven rows of whitish colored teeth.

"Leave me alone, Carrie."

"So...Leslie?"

"If she was Leslie, she would have already hit you with something," Nadia commented from the seat across from me.

"Or stabbed you," I added, reminding myself not to laugh at her shock. I couldn't let myself take Leslie lightly.

"True." She put her finger against her pointy chin. "Since its you, you wanna game of cards?"

I glanced around her to Janice, who didn't seem as welcoming. "I...think I'll sit out today," I swallowed hard. "These new pills they have me on make my fingers shake anyways."

"Whatever," Carrie shrugged and pranced away to join Janice.

"What pills do they have you on?" Nadia snatched my hand from the table before I could pull it away. She searched it with careful eyes, as if she were looking for the cause of their shaking.

"I don't know what they're called." I sighed deeply, knowing what Beth would have said about me taking new medicine that I knew nothing about. "But I know they help."

"How do you know that?" She dropped my hand back down. "Making your hands shake like that doesn't seem helpful," she scowled.

"I know because," I twisted my hands tightly together, "my name is Mellie again."

"There's that bitch," someone yelled from across the room.

I turned in my seat, wondering idly who would fight today. A girl I had never seen before, who was easily three times my size, was pointing her stubby finger directly at me. "You, she boomed.

"Me?" My heart sped up. I really hoped she didn't mean me.

"Yeah, you," she growled, moving across the room to get closer to my table.

Shrinking back in my seat, I shot a horrified glance to Nadia. "Who is that?" I hissed.

"Her name is Joe," Nadia supplied. "They say she went crazy on a group of preppy girls at her school. Killed them all."

"What?" Maybe I could crawl under the table, she probably wouldn't be able to reach me there.

"She probably just told people that to make everyone scared of her."

"What did I tell you, skinny bitch?" Joe demanded angrily, stopping just short of barreling me over.

"I..." I shook my head slowly, "I have no idea."

"She said if she saw you in here again, you'd be sorry," Carrie very kindly reminded me. There was a cackle of laughter but I kept my eyes on Joe in case she decided to start swinging.

"I just go where they tell me," my voice shook.

"Back off, Bertha," Nadia called out. At some point she had stood up from the table and come around to my side, putting herself far too close to the angry Joe.

"Don't. Call. Me. Bertha." Joe's nostrils flared wide with each word.

My entire body shaking now, I rose up to put myself between the two girls. "I'm sure she just forgot your name," I tried to smile.

"No, I didn't," Nadia shrugged. "Bertha just fits you better."

"What did you say?" Joe flared up, making her shoulders go even wider.

"What? Were those words too long for you to understand?"

"Nadia," I widened my eyes at her. "What are you doing?"

"I just want to be sure that Bertha understands me."

Carrie laughed wildly.

Joe lunged forward but I managed to move myself and Nadia out of the way just in time. She fell into the table and thudded to the ground.

"Whoa," Nadia whopped, "you're gonna break the table, Bertha."

"Stop it," I hissed, elbowing past Nadia to try and help Joe up. "Are you ok?" I asked nervously.

"You stupid bitch," she cried out. Moving faster than I would have given her credit for, she swung her fist upwards and punched me in the face.

Chaos broke out.

I fell backwards. Nadia jumped at Joe. Joe swung her arms and legs to hit anything close enough. The girls around us laughed and yelled. I scrambled to separate the two again. Then the nurses came with their angry frowns and needles.

"You should have just stayed back," Nadia grunted. A nurse had her knee pressed into her back.

My mouth wouldn't stay closed – either from shock or the swelling from getting punched so hard, I couldn't tell. "She wasn't even after you."

"She wasn't after you either."

"Yes she was."

"She was after Leslie."

Leslie.

~

It had been a long time since I had cried over being put in solitary, but once the tears started falling I couldn't stop them. I had spent so long being controlled by Leslie; now it was hard knowing what to do next. How had I made decisions before Leslie appeared in the rain that day?

Without meaning to – I missed her.

Almost every part of me was sorry I had ever met her. Then there was a small part that was terrified to be without her. I had grown used to Leslie telling me what to do and what to wear and what to eat.

Knowing I would be in the small room for a while, I curled onto my side and laid down on the floor. Maybe I would get lucky and be able to fall asleep until the nurses came.

My thoughts shifted slightly to Nadia. Leslie told me she was friends with Ethan but I didn't know if I believed that or not. She was nothing like the usual girl he went for. She stuck up for me against Joe – to the point that she was locked in a room similar to mine.

Why had she done that, I found myself wondering. The only thing Nadia knew about me was what Leslie had shown her. I cringed against the wall and sucked in my bottom lip. People weren't nice to you unless they wanted something from you – Leslie had taught me that – so what did Nadia want from me?

I let my eyelids flutter closed. Sleep wouldn't come easily but maybe...

~

"At least it's something you can recognize today, huh?" Nurse Kaydee grinned nervously at me and then down to my plate of food.

"Cheeseburger," I grunted, smiling for her benefit. My lips were shaking almost as much as my hands.

"Do you want me to try and sneak you some extra ketchup?" she asked in a low voice. I nodded quickly up at her.

"Was that nurse giving you a hard time?" Nadia asked, sliding onto the bench across from me.

"No," I sighed. "She's getting me some more ketchup."

"Hmmm," her eyes narrowed suspiciously, reminding me of Leslie.

Nurse Kaydee returned with a packet of ketchup, a look of triumph lighting her face. "Success!"

"Thanks," I chuckled.

"I'm not sure it's a good idea for the two of you to be sitting together," her smile changed quickly to a frown when she looked at Nadia.

"There's no assigned seats," Nadia scowled.

"Considering your history..."

"I don't like Leslie," Nadia shrugged, "I'm still deciding on Mellie."

Nurse Kaydee hesitated, on the verge of arguing, but a loud crash across the room caught her attention. "No trouble with you two." She pointed at each of us in turn before hurrying away.

"Trouble," Nadia scoffed. "What can we do in here?" She was still scowling as she bit into her sandwich.

"Trouble does have a nasty way of finding me." I took a small bite and chewed slowly. I actually didn't like ketchup but how could I argue with Nurse Kaydee's excitement?

"Yeah, because of Leslie."

"You do know we're the same person, right?" She was always quick to separate me and Leslie but that wasn't often possible. Especially when it came to the consequences I had to pay for Leslie's actions.

"Yeah, but..." she shrugged again.

"What's your brand of crazy?" I asked bluntly.

"It was self defense."

"What happened?"

"He took me out on a date and got pissed when I wouldn't give it up to him."

"So you killed him?" I could feel my eyes widen. She was too much like Leslie, I was going to have to make sure other people could see her.

"No." She put her cheeseburger back on her plate. "He got rough and I was just trying to get away. I pushed him and he hit his head on some rocks. Next thing I knew, I was locked up in a jail cell. I was so freaked out in there that the judge decided to send me here until they figure out what to do."

"How long have you been here?"

Nadia took a long breath. "Almost six months."

"That's a long time to figure things out. It's not like it was your fault."

"Well...someone is dead and it was because of my hands." She let her breath out through her nose. "That's a lot to deal with."

"Yeah." I knew what that felt like.

"What did you do?"

"I killed Ethan Sturgis." I took another small bite, preparing for her to freak out again.

"No shit?" She picked up her discarded food. "I heard about that, I didn't know that was you though."

"Leslie said you knew him," I said, carefully avoiding eye contact.

"He dated my cousin for a few weeks one summer," her shoulder bobbed, "and she drug me to a few of those house parties by the lake. We weren't exactly close."

"He dated everyone for a few weeks," I laughed nervously.

"Not me," her eyes went briefly wide. "Did you ever go to any of those parties?"

"Some."

"No shit?"

I laughed again.

"We might have seen each other."

"Leslie saw you once."

"That's crazy," she mumbled around a full mouth. "My mom always says the world is small, guess she's right. So did you know a girl named Becca...something? I can't remember her last name."

"Are you talking about Becca Miller? Pretty blonde girl with a giant stick up her butt?"

"Yes," Nadia laughed loudly. "So this one time..."

I sat back more comfortably, amazed at this unexpected connection to the outside world. I would have to tell Leslie that Nadia wasn't actually friends with Ethan after all. No, I amended my thoughts quickly, I wasn't going to be telling Leslie anything.

~

"Do you think..." I licked my bottom lip, unsure how to ask Dr. Simmons anything. She was Leslie's friend, not mine.

"Do I think what?" She smiled wide, waiting.

"Do you think it's ok for me to...be friends with someone?"

"Someone in here, you mean?"

Obviously, where else would I be able to meet someone? I thought doctors were supposed to be smart. "Yeah."

"Do you want a friend?"

"Maybe."

"I'll be your friend." Her teeth flashed white.

"I don't mean you," I scowled, feeling my eyebrows pucker.

Her smile didn't falter. "Then who do you mean?"

"A girl named Nadia."

It was clear by the disappearance of teeth that Leslie had talked about Nadia to Dr. Simmons. "I know Leslie didn't like her, but I think she's alright."

"What do you like about her?"

"Well...she knew some of the same people I knew so when I talk to her – I don't feel as crazy as this place makes me feel." Did that make sense? Was it even a complete sentence? "And she doesn't see me as Leslie."

"How does it make you feel to be seen separate from Leslie?"

"Did you and Dr. Matthews go to the same school?" My nose scrunched up slightly.

"Why do you ask?" she grinned broadly.

"You say the same things." I didn't return her smile. "He always wants to know how I feel."

"I suppose it's just because we want to make sure you're ok."

"So...what do you think?"

"About your feelings?"

"No," I blinked several times. I really couldn't make myself like Dr. Simmons; maybe it was because Leslie liked her. "About me having a friend."

"Nadia."

"Well...I mean..." I pulled at a piece of skin on my finger. "Just in general. Do you think it's possible for someone like me to have a friend, I mean."

"Of course it's possible." Although she smiled, it didn't quite reach her eyes.

She was lying, but maybe I was desperate enough to go ahead and believe her anyways.

"You'll let me know how things go with Nadia, right?"

"Sure." My shoulders slumped forward. Why did she have to go and make things weird?

~

Twisting my fingers nervously together, I scanned the day room for Nadia. I knew it wasn't smart, but I wanted to be friends with her. I was ready to feel a little bit normal again.

"Mellie!"

Turning my head, I spotted her – waving her hand at me from a table by the window. Careful not to look at the window seat, I hurried over and sank gratefully down into the empty chair. "I was looking for you," I gushed, grinning.

"I'm not really hard to find," she rolled her eyes dramatically. "I'm the crazy blonde with a boy hair cut."

Laughter bubbled up out of my throat. "You need to get that printed on a tee shirt."

"My mom probably wouldn't appreciate the humor." She pulled a puzzle box from the small pile next to the table. "Fancy a jigsaw?" she asked in a high pitched British accent.

The picture on the box was a small grey kitten with a butterfly on it's nose. Safe – and more importantly, it wasn't one that me and Leslie had done. "Sure," I nodded a little too excitedly.

"I'm sure it won't be as thrilling as you're anticipating." She pried the lid off the top and poured all the pieces out on the table.

I clicked my tongue against the roof of my mouth. "You can't do it like this," I scowled. "We need to take all the edge pieces out first."

"We need to do the cat first," she tsked back, "then work our way out."

"You're absolutely crazy." Despite her protests, I scooped the puzzle back into the box and started sorting out the edge pieces. "You put together the frame," I ordered.

"Whatever you say," she rolled her eyes. "I had no idea you were a puzzle genius."

Surprising myself, I laughed again. "Well, now you know."

"Tonight is movie night," she commented after putting together a few random pieces.

"Yeah?" Movie night was optional – and a privledge. Not everyone got to go.

"Are you going?"

My hands froze. "I don't know." I had never went before; Leslie didn't like the movie theater because they turned off all the lights. "What are they playing?"

Nadia shrugged. "I'm sure it'll be some bull shit movie where they sing too much and smile over leaves falling."

"They do show a lot of kids movies." I continued sorting pieces. "Are you going?"

"I'll go if you go. We can make fun of it together."

"That sounds like...fun, actually."

"Fun might be too strong of a word." She glanced over the edge pieces, looking for something to fit the small line she had going. "But it's better than sitting alone in our rooms."

"I'll ask Nurse Kaydee if I can go," I grinned over at her.

"You better. I'm gonna be pissed if I get there and you don't show up."

"You can always sit with Carrie." I couldn't help but laugh at the look of disgust she threw me.

~

I swallowed thickly, anticpating the moment they would turn the lights off. "What are they playing again?" I whispered nervously to Nadia.

Nurse Kaydee had seemed as surprised as I was by my sudden request to join movie night. But she smiled and conceded easily enough, encouraging me "to go be normal". I wasn't sure that this qualified. Still, I sighed, it was worth a shot.

"Mary Poppins," she grinned.

"Everyone likes that movie," I attempted a smile back. It might have gotten lost on the way to my face though because Nadia looked suddenly concerned.

"Are you ok?"

"Yes," I squeaked quickly. I cleared my throat and tried again. "I haven't seen a movie in a really long time," I confided. "Not since I came here."

"How long have you been here?"

"No idea."

Her eyes widened; I couldn't blame her. "You really don't know how long you've been locked up?"

"I would guess eight or nine years," I shrugged. "But you kind of loose track."

"How old are you?"

Why did she have to keep asking me questions that made me sound like a crazy person. "I don't know," I hissed, keeping my eyes on the screen. "I think I came here when I was nineteen, maybe twenty."

"Doesn't it bother you?" she asked in a different sort of voice, a tone that made me look at her again. She was staring at me, her huge eyes filled with liquid.

"You're not going to cry, are you?"

"Your life is passing by and you don't even remember most of it," she continued morosely.

"I have to stay here until..."

"Until what?"

"Until Leslie goes away."

"What if she never goes away?"

"Dr. Matthews said..."

"But what if he's wrong," she cut me off. "What if Leslie doesn't go away."

"I'll get stronger," I nodded firmly. "I'll become stronger than Leslie, then I can leave here." I couldn't start doubting myself now.

"You're never going to be stronger than me," a familiar voice purred from the seat behind me.

Whirling around in my seat, I came face to face with Leslie. "What are you doing here?" I whispered, horrified by the changes in her. Dark circles under her eyes made her look like the scary girl from The Ring; not that I ever watched scary movies. I accidently saw a preview once though.

Leslie laughed softly. "Long time no see, Mellie."

"Who are you talking to?" Nadia turned to mimick my backwards stare.

"Nadia," Leslie hissed. Her top lip peeled away from her teeth.

"I think I'll go back to my room," I panted, my heart racing.

"The movie hasn't even started yet," Nadia protested.

"She doesn't wanna watch a movie with you," Leslie suddenly yelled.

Shrinking back in her seat, Nadia watched me – waiting.

"We are not friends." Leslie took one hand and shoved hard at Nadia's shoulder.

"Stop it," I warned her, trying not to move my lips when I talked. "We're leaving."

"I'm not going anywhere." Leslie slammed back against her seat and crossed her arms tightly over her chest. "I want to watch this movie with my new BFF."

"Leslie..."

"Leslie is here?" Nadia's face went pale. "Do you actually see her?"

"We...I mean I..." I ran my tongue across my bottom lip. "It was a bad idea to come here."

"I'm. Not. Leaving." Leslie snarled. She leaned forward until her face was close to Nadia's head.

"What are you doing?"

"I"m sitting," she grunted. "Obviously."

"Leave her alone."

"Mellie?"

I backed out into the isle. Where were the nurses when you actually needed them? "I'm fine," I assured Nadia with a plastic voice. "Just tired."

"Tired," Leslie snorted. "What a stupid thing to say."

"Why can't you just leave me alone?"

"Why would I do that?" She flung backwards and laid her head on the seat until she was looking up at the ceiling.

"I'm leaving. You have to leave if I do."

"Do you know what I think is funny?" She moved her head slowly, raising it so she could smile at me.

"What?" I probably didn't want to know.

"You have no idea right now if you're me...or you." She moved her finger to point between the two of us. "Are you standing or sitting?" She giggled loudly, the sound echoing.

"I'm...I'm standing." Wasn't I standing? Leslie couldn't control me that much, right? I looked to Nadia. She was staring at me, her mouth hanging slightly open; but she was looking at me...not Leslie. "They can't see you," I declared triumphantly.

"What are you talking about, Mellie?" Nadia asked, leaning towards me. "Should I get the nurse?"

"You are not friends with this bitch!" Suddenly enraged, Leslie shot out and grabbed a fistful of Nadia's hair.

She wasn't the real one though, knowing that made me strong enough. I turned away from the pair of them and hurried out of the theater. Leslie couldn't do anything without me. She was nothing.

"Nothing huh?" Out in the hallway, Leslie popped up in front of me and slammed into my body. Unable to correct my balance, I fell to the floor. I didn't even try to stop the wild laughter that bubbled up out of my throat.

"You had to leave," I gasped, taking in a breath between my barks of laughter. "You couldn't stay there without me."

"So?" Her face twisted in rage.

"So?" I rolled onto my back, still panting and laughing. "That means that I. Am. Stronger. Than. You."

"Mellie?" Nurse Kaydee's face appeared over me. "Are you alright?"

"I don't know," I cried. "But maybe."

~

"I don't know why you're so happy," Leslie grumbled. She had her arms wrapped around the middle of her stomach, making her look frailer than usual.

"I...just am," I shrugged. My feet dangled off the edge of the couch.

"It's not that big of a deal."

"I made you go away," I reminded her in a sing song voice.

"You didn't make me do anything."

"You just don't want to admit that I'm stronger than you..."

"You're not stronger than me," she violently hissed.

"...than you thought I was," I finished.

"One time." She held up one long finger.

Despite her glare, I grinned even wider.

She leaned forward. "I think you're missing the most important thing." She grinned too, but it didn't look happy.

"What's the most important thing?"

"You can see me now."

My grin slipped a little at the corners. "What?"

"You can see me," she repeated slowly.

"I've seen you for a long time."

"That means," she tapped the side of her head, "that those green pills aren't working anymore."

"That's not entirely true," Dr. Matthews spoke up from his silent seat across the room from us.

"Those pills," Leslie smiled sweetly at him, "are supposed to keep me away." She flung her arms wide, pointing out the obvious. She was still here.

"Medicine is incredibly helpful when dealing with mental illness," Dr. Matthews countered gently, "but it will only work when combined with other things."

"What other things?" Leslie scowled.

"Therepy is one."

"Pfft, you just don't want to admit that you can't help her."

"That's not true," I threw my own arms wide to block Leslie from his view. "I left the theater and she had to follow me. She couldn't hurt anyone. The pills have to be working."

"That wasn't the medicine," he smiled, "that was you getting stronger."

"Don't be putting ideas in her head." Leslie stormed across the room and kicked the trash can, but it didn't fall over.

~

Hands clasped tightly together, I set them on the table in front of me. I had given up trying to finish my oatmeal after Leslie knocked the spoon from my hand three times. Puffing my cheeks out to the furthest extent, I let the air blow through my lips very slowly.

"Hey," Leslie slammed her fist on the table. "Why aren't you eating?"

I pressed my lips tight together. I wasn't going to answer her and I wasn't going to let her talk through me. Not anymore.

"You're not hungry?" She shoved the bowl closer to my closed hands. "That stupid nurse isn't going to let you get away with not eating."

Opening my eyes just slightly, I pushed my held breath back out of my lungs. Nurse Kaydee hardly ever tried to force me to eat these days, not since I woke up again. I wasn't going to cause a scene though.

That's exactly what Leslie wanted.

"Hey," Leslie screamed, smacking the table again. "Don't ignore me."

"Hey." I jumped at the sound of Nadia's voice. "I heard that Janice is freaking out this morning," her eyes were bright with poorly concealed excitement.

"Why?" I breathed, barely able to get the word out past my nerves. Leslie was glaring at Nadia, obviously planning something bad.

"I guess the nurse found her hair collection," Nadia laughed behind her closed fist.

"She has a hair collection?"

"Apparently," Nadia shrugged. "Why aren't you eating," she thrust her chin in the direction of my untouched tray.

"I'm not hungry."

"It doesn't taste any worse than usual," she declared around a mouthful of mush.

"Leslie's here." I wasn't sure what made me tell her, I immediately wished I could take the words back. They were already out there though.

Nadia's fork froze halfway to her mouth. "What?"

"She's sitting right next to you." Nadia turned to face what must have just been empty space to her. Leslie waved with two fingers.

"Hey Nadia," she sang.

"She can't hear you."

"Leslie can't hear me?" Nadia looked back at me, her eyebrows bunched together.

"No, I..." I sucked in a quick breath and focused on the person who was actually real. "Did the nurses take her hair?" I plastered a wide smile on my face, hoping I looked interested and not crazy.

Nadia carefully put her fork down on her plate. "Is Leslie giving you a hard time?"

Without any warning, my eyes filled with burning tears. How long had it been since I cried? Maybe it had been years or maybe it was just that morning. Time was a tricky thing these days. "I'm just not sure what she's going to do to you," I whispered. "She doesn't seem to like you."

"I don't like her either," Nadia sat back with a huff. "This is so weird."

"I know." One tear escaped and slid slowly down my face. Nadia wouldn't want to be my friend now. Leslie's doctor was wrong, a person like me couldn't have a friend. It wasn't possible.

"Why would you want a friend like her anyways?" Leslie suddenly screamed. "She was friends with Ethan to - are you missing him now? Wouldn't it be nice if the three of you could have a picnic together?" Her lips curled up off the top of her teeth.

"I wasn't friends with Ethan," Nadia fired back.

The color drained from my face. "You can hear Leslie?"

"It's kind of easy to tell when you're being Leslie," she glared at me. But you can tell that bitch that I wasn't friends with Ethan Sturgis."

I turned to Leslie. "She says..."

"I heard her," she growled. "I saw her with him. I know they were friends."

"What did she say?"

"I..."

"Don't speak for me." Leslie jumped up from the table. "Don't you dare think you're stronger than me." She took one arm and swung it across the table, sending both trays crashing into Nadia's lap.

Shocked, Nadia shot up too. "What the hell," she shrieked.

"I don't think she believes you," I choked.

"She's lying," Leslie thundered.

The cafeteria had gone strangely quiet so the sound echoed back to my ears like a roar. "Don't call me a liar," Nadia was facing me, her mouth clenched tight.

Without meaning to, I must have let Leslie talk through me again. "Leave her alone," I hissed to Leslie, trying not to move my lips when I talked.

"Funny thing." When Leslie turned to me, nothing about her face suggested funny. "I remember telling you almost the same exact thing; and yet here you are." She flung her arm at the table. "Eating breakfast with your new best friend. No wonder you think you don't need me anymore."

"What's going on over here?" one of the nurses barked out, coming over to investigate.

"We're going to have to go to the hole again," I hissed to Leslie. "Stop causing a scene."

"Ha," she huffed loudly. "I'm not even here," she's simpered in a baby voice, "remember Mellie?"

"Stop it."

"This is all you."

All around us, the people in the cafeteria were staring. Nadia watched me with narrowed eyes; it was hard to look at her. "Don't look at Mellie like that." Suddenly wild again, Leslie lunged for Nadia.

"I already told you not to do that," I screamed, forgetting the nurse in my desperation to control Leslie.

"Why do you always get attached to strays?" Leslie changed direction and came at me instead.

Taken by surprise, I fell backwards. The hard concrete bit at my elbows and the palms of my hands.

"Mellie!" Nadia took a step towards me but Leslie pushed her back.

"Don't touch her!"

"That's enough," nurse Kaydee called above the chaos. "Everyone back to your tables." I couldn't see past nurse Kaydee's bulk over me - I heard the shuffle of feet as people obeyed her command. "Back to your room, Parker," she growled. "No more breakfast for you."

"I hate the oatmeal here anyway," I panted.

Somewhere over my shoulder, Leslie snorted loudly.

~

"Mellie," Nurse Kaydee's sturdy form stood in the doorway of my room, blocking out most of the light from the hallway, "I talked to Dr. Matthews."

I didn't move my head to look up at her. Did she think I cared what he had to say? Besides - I already knew.

"He thinks it would be best to keep you away from the general population."

Of course he did.

"He believes that it's best for your safety... "

...and the safety of others...

"... and the safety of others." Nurse Kaydee hesitated. "He did say that you're allowed to stay in your own room this time though."

I pressed my lips tight together, refusing to talk to her. Couldn't she just hurry up and go away?

As if she could hear my unfriendly thoughts, she turned away without another word. I saw the light from the hall only for a moment before the door closed and I was left by myself.

Sort of.

"Well," Leslie squatted near the wall, "this is better than the hole."

"I guess," I shrugged my shoulders.

"I don't get why you're pissed."

"You attacked Nadia."

"You're not seriously thinking of being her friend?" Leslie sputtered

Rolling my eyes, I let my legs fall back onto the bed. "I was thinking about it - yeah."

"Stop thinking about it." She slid down further until she was sitting on the ground.

"I want a friend, Leslie."

"You have me."

"You're not real."

"I'm real to you."

"You hurt people."

"Most people deserve it."

I pressed my lips tight together. This was what Leslie did - she pulled me away from everyone else. She wanted me to feel alone so I would keep coming back to her.

It wasn't working this time though. No matter what, I had to get out of this place. I really didn't want to live my whole life locked away.

"You're always going to need me, Mellie," Leslie taunted softly.

I took a deep breath and let it out slowly through my nose. "Maybe, but maybe not."

~

"So," a young woman that I had never seen before pressed her hands together and pushed them against her chin, "welcome to group everyone. My name is Lori."

"Are you old enough to be a doctor?" Carrie snarled.

"You don't look it," Janice echoed.

"Well, I'm not a doctor..."

"Then why are they making us talk to you?" Janice cut her off.

"I'm a counselor," her smile turned rigid but didn't disappear.

"Like from school?" A new girl called Monica asked.

"No. I'm... I'm not from a school."

"I'm not talking to you," Carrie declared, crossing her arms over small chest.

"Neither are we," Leslie seconded, raising her hand. "We only talk to real doctors."

"I'm Mellie," I said quickly, glaring at Leslie. "I'm here because I shot Ethan Sturgis."

Beside me, Nadia slapped her hand over her mouth to muffle her laughter. "I'm Nadia," she choked after a moment. "I also killed someone."

"Me too," Janice raised her hand, grinning wide.

"Well, I did too," Carrie was quick to add.

"Okay," Lori raised both hands in front of her, looking slightly alarmed. "We're not here to talk about the past."

"I thought we could talk about what we wanted," Nadia spoke up.

"You... you can."

"I want to talk about murder," Janice smiled at Lori. "Can we talk about that?"

"Have you ever killed someone, Lori?" Monica asked.

"No, of course not."

"Then she'd be locked up in here," Carrie scowled.

"Have you ever wanted to kill anyone?" Janice asked.

"No."

"She answered that way too fast," Leslie let her eyes go wide. "You've thought about it, haven't you Lori?"

"I would never..."

"You have thought about it though," Leslie purred, "thought about what it would feel like to watch someone take their last breath."

The circle had gone quiet. Everyone was watching Leslie and Lori.

"We're going to talk about controlling our anger today," Lori forcibly made her voice calm. "What are some of the things that make you angry?"

Swallowing past the lump in my throat, I was the first to answer her. "It makes me mad when the nurses try to force me to eat," I said softly.

The counselor, who was not a doctor and not in school, watched me wearily. After an extremely awkward silence, she nodded.

"It pisses me off when they make us do group," Carrie sneered.

"Especially with a kindergarten teacher," Janice nodded.

"All right," Lori rolled her eyes. It was becoming clear what made her angry. "So how do we handle that anger?"

"Kill them," Nadia was the first to say. There was a shuffle of laughter around the circle.

From her chair across from me, Leslie glared at me.

Ignoring her completely, I looked at Nadia. "This lady is such a joke," she snorted.

~

"Here," I set the square box on the table between me and Nadia, "this looks like a new one."

"Are you sure?" She frowned down at the puzzle with the three horses on it.

"Yeah." I pulled the box across the table. "I've done all these puzzles at least twice - except this one."

"It doesn't matter," Nadia sighed. "We're young - puzzles are for old ladies."

"And crazy people."

Nadia rolled her eyes dramatically. "If we weren't here right now," she popped the lid off the puzzle, "what would you be doing?"

"Probably just be in my room." I sifted my fingers through the loose pieces.

"I mean," she sighed, "if you weren't locked up in here."

I knew what she meant. But I didn't like to think of things like that. Hope, I had learned, was a tricky thing.

"I think that..." I began to pull out the edge pieces, being careful not to look up at Nadia. What if she laughed? I mean - it did sound kind of childish. "I would like to own a flower shop."

"I didn't know you liked flowers."

"They're pretty," I shrugged, "and they're quiet."

"They are quiet," Nadia chuckled.

"My mom had a garden and I used to love growing things."

"Yeah?"

"Yeah," I nodded. "Working with flowers would be amazing."

"Did you see that list in the Career counciling room?"

There was a Career counciling room? "No."

"I'm pretty sure Horticulture was on there."

"I've never been in there, they must not think I'll be able to do a career."

Nadia shook her head. "They give you classes when you get ready to leave here. You could take that class Mellie, and get to work with flowers."

I didn't look at her, I couldn't. My heart was hammering too hard. Although I hadn't given it permission to, my heart was starting to hope.

"What about you?" I asked after clearing my throat. "What do you want to do if you have a future?"

"Everyone has a future." She picked out several pieces. "Maybe there will be a cute little nail shop down the road from your flower shop," she grinned.

"Nails," my nose scrunched up.

"Yeah," she held up one hand. "I used to love getting my nails done. Me and my mom..." Her words fell away.

My own mother had never taken me to get my nails done - not once. To be fair, she never got her own done either. I glanced down at my hands. The nails were jagged where I bit them; the skin was peeled and cracked. If I did get my nails done, I'd be embarrassed show them to anyone.

"So you'll just paint nails all day?"

"There's probably more to it than that," she scowled playfully. "Getting your nails done is something normal - I want to be part of something normal."

That made perfect sense, actually. After the years I had spent inside a looney bin - normal sounded so perfect. There was just one catch for me though.

And she was sitting across the room, next to the window.

Leslie grinned and waved at me. "Having fun?" she called.

Taking a deep breath, I turned back to the puzzle. What was the point of plans with Nadia when I was stuck in here with Leslie? And maybe I would be stuck with her forever.

"Here," Nadia slid a line of pieces to me, "these go with the sky."

~

"What has you troubled today?" Dr. Matthews asked calmly after several tense minutes of silence had passed.

"Nothing," I jumped at the question, instantly defensive. "I'm just here talking to you."

"Yes."

"They force me to."

"Don't you like talking to me?"

I pressed my lips tight together. "I don't like being forced to do everything. I want to get out of here."

Dr. Matthews nodded slowly. "Are you still seeing Leslie?"

Out of the corner of my eye, I peered at the seat next to me. "Sometimes," I admitted through my closed teeth.

"Does she tell you what to do?"

"Yeah." How many times was he going to ask the same questions?

"Do you ever listen to her?"

My nostrils flared. "I think you need to get some new material, doc," I snapped. "You just asked me this yesterday."

"And you said?"

I threw myself back against the couch. "Whatever." It was hard to not listen to Leslie - she always got right in my face and screamed. Who wouldn't listen to her?

To his credit, Dr. Matthews didn't smile - he was used to my fits. "Is this what has you upset today? Has Leslie told you to do something?"

"No," Leslie snapped before I could respond.

"Not really," I echoed, just after her outburst.

"Not really?" she squealed.

"I was talking to Nadia..."

"Oh here we go with Nadia." Leslie threw her hands up.

"What were you two talking about?" Dr. Matthews asked patiently.

"About the career center." I couldn't keep the accusing growl from my voice. He had never let me go into the career center.

"What about the career center?"

"I didn't even know it existed," I shot out angrily.

"It wasn't time yet for you."

"But it is for Nadia?" My bottom lip jutted out, in full pout mode. "She got here after me."

"Every case is different."

"You like her better than me, don't you?" What did she have that I didn't? Why was she better than me?

"You know that isn't true," he told me calmly.

I threw my arm across my face. "Obviously, you think she has a future and I don't."

"Everyone has a future."

"Is that what they teach in the *career center*, because that's what Nadia said to."

"What would you like to do, Mellie?"

"I'd like to..." I hesitated. But Dr. Matthews wouldn't make fun of me. "I want to take those flower classes. I want to have a flower shop."

"Seems like a sensible goal," he nodded and scribbled across his page.

"No," Leslie snarled out. "We're not taking any stupid classes."

"They aren't stupid," I hissed back to her. "Tell her they aren't stupid."

Dr. Matthews watched me through his wise eyes, eyes I'd come to know well over the years. He never liked when I wanted him to talk to Leslie. I really wished I would remember that.

~

The warm water washed over the top of my head and down the length of my slender body. Along the cracked tile by my feet, there was a steady stream of mostly clean water.

Other than the nurse standing right outside the door, I was alone in the shower room. It was highly unusual to be able to take a shower alone in this place. I leaned my face upwards, reveling in the feel of the water pressure against my skin.

If I closed my eyes tight enough, I could almost remember what it was like before I got locked away. If I was home, mom would be pounding on the bathroom door soon. She was convinced that long showers were bad for your skin. *You won't be young forever, Melody,* her voice snapped from one of the dark corners of my mind. *You need to take better care of your skin.*

Intense sadness suddenly washed over me, stronger than the stream of quickly cooling water. If mom had come to visit me while Leslie was in charge...

I shuddered at the thought. Leslie hated my mom, I could only imagine the horrible things she had said to her when I wasn't around to stop her.

For the first time in a very long time, I wanted my mom. It was strange - but true. What I wouldn't give to hear her nagging at me.

"If you're not careful, you're going to turn into blubbering mess," Leslie growled out angrily.

I jumped at the sound of her voice. "I didn't know you were here," I sputtered through the water.

"That's because your eyes were closed." She crossed her arms over her chest. "What were you dreaming about, Sleeping Beauty?"

"None of your business," I shivered slightly.

Leslie clicked her tongue against the roof of her mouth three times. "Mellie,"she wagged her finger at me, "I really don't like how rude you've gotten. I think it's your new friends - they aren't a good influence on you."

Despite standing under the water, my mouth felt extremely dry. It was hard to swallow, words wouldn't come to me.

"What do you think we should do about that?"

"You could just leave me alone," I suggested hoarsely.

"No." Her arms dropped to her sides.

I took a step back, there wasn't far to go. A solid wall blocked my path away from her. "What are you going to do?"

Leslie glared at me through slitted eyes. "It didn't have to be this way."

"What way?" My heart was hammering.

"I didn't want you to be afraid of me."

Should I call for the nurse?

"We were once best friends."

"You hurt people." I tried to keep the whimper out of my voice. "And you were never real."

She threw her fist out to the side, punching the wall. The thud echoed through the shower room. "I get so sick of hearing those words," she rasped. "I. Am. Real."

I couldn't talk so I just shook my head from side to side.

"You know what real feels like, Mellie?"

"Yeah," my voice shook. I had seen Leslie mad before - she was always mad, but it had never been so directed at me before.

"How about I show you." She moved in a flash. Before I could even blink my eyes, she was right in my face.

"What are you..."

In the same quick movements, she grabbed my head in her two hands and thrust it backwards - straight into the concrete wall.

My scream echoed throughout the room. "Stop it," I pleaded.

She didn't listen. Over and over again she sent my head into the wall, until the stream of water by my feet ran red.

Until finally, the nurse ran into the room. "What are you doing?" she shrieked.

The arrival of the nurse startled Leslie enough to let me go. Terrified and dizzy, I crawled naked across the blood-soaked floor. I didn't get far before Leslie jumped on me again.

"Is this real enough?" she roared. "Does this feel *real* to you?"

"Stop," the nurse screamed. "Backup in shower room three," she panted into her radio. "I need backup in here! Melody Parker... She... I... I need backup!"

Blood ran into my eyes, making everything red and blurry. Leslie didn't let go of me until more nurses showed up - armed with needles that turned the red room to darkness.

~

It was clear as soon as I opened my eyes that I was laying in a bed - not in my room. The stark white ceiling above me was lined with two long light bulbs.

I couldn't move - they had tied my hands down to the bed. Moving my head was painful. Had they tied my head down to?

Managing to move enough to see the machine by the bed, I realized where I was. I was in the hospital. But why...

My heart sped up as memories flooded over me. Leslie had attacked me when I was taking a shower. She had bashed my head into the wall. That's why I couldn't move it very well.

Leslie tried to kill me.

My eyes scanned the part of the room that I could actually see. I expected her to be there - glaring at me for not dying. She wasn't there though - no one was there.

I yanked hard at my hand restraints. If I just stayed laying there, she would come back to finish me off.

"Hey," I tried to scream. My voice was raspy - my throat felt like fire from even that small effort. "Is someone out there," I coughed. A nurse had to be somewhere close by. In all the years I'd been there, they were never far.

"You're awake?"

As if in slow motion, I turned my face towards the sound of the voice. "Yeah," I gasped. A woman I didn't recognize stood over my bed holding a clipboard.

"How does your head feel?" She grabbed my eyelids and forced my eyes open wide so she could peer into them with her tiny flashlight.

"It's...um..." It didn't hurt, it just felt heavy. "I'm fine. Will you untie my hands?"

"No," she answered bluntly, not unkind.

"I don't want to stay in this bed." I pulled again at the restraints.

"Dr. Matthews will be in soon to talk to you." Ignoring my protests, she turned and left the room.

"Wait." The door clicked shut with a deafening silence.

There was nothing I could do about the restraints. Although my mind tried to race ahead and plan an escape, I knew I had to appear calm. Dr. Matthews would be coming - he would be the one to take the restraints off. If I was acting crazy, he would make me stay.

I took a deep breath and let it out as slowly as possible. While my eyes were still closed, the door creaked open again.

"Mellie?" Nurse Kaydee called out softly.

"I'm awake." I raised my head up as far as possible to be sure she knew I was awake.

"How are you feeling?" She pushed the hair off my forehead. "You got pretty banged up in there." Worry chased pity all over her face.

"I'm fine," I hurried to assure her. "But you have to get them to take these off." I wiggled my hands. "The other lady said Dr. Matthews would be coming in. Where is he?"

"He'll be right in." Before she even finished her sentence, the door opened yet again. Dr. Matthew was suddenly there, looking down at me, next to nurse Kaydee.

"Welcome back Mellie," he smiled gently. "Is Leslie here?"

"No." I hadn't searched the entire room but she wasn't in my clear sight.

He nodded his head in approval. "That's good."

'Can I get out of here now," I hissed, "before she comes back."

Above my head, Nurse and Doctor exchanged a dark look. My forehead creased. What did that mean?

"Leslie has become violent," Dr. Matthews said slowly. "Are you afraid of her?"

"I've always been a little scared," I whimpered. "She attacked me."

"It could have been a lot worse." Nurse Kaydee's lips thinned out.

I was tied to hospital bed, my head was bruised and bleeding, and Dr. Matthews had never looked darker. How much worse could things get?

"Can I go back to my room?"

"We're going to increase some of your meds," he said in place of a real answer. "We'll see if that helps."

"You can't leave me here." My voice rose, the false calm was slipping. "Please!"

"You're safe here."

"No," I jerked hard at the unmoving restraints. "Let me go with you, don't leave me."

"I'll come back to check on you in the morning," nurse Kaydee patted my shoulder awkwardly.

"No!"

It didn't matter how loud I screamed or how hard I bucked my body, no one came back for me. My cries echoed in the room. "Help me," I gasped. "Please help me!"

~

"Still alive?" A voice taunted from the thin slot in the metal door.

I pressed my lips tight together and huddled closer to the soft wall.

"You best answer," the voice jeered, "or I'll have to send someone down to collect your dead body." The flap banged open and closed several times.

"I'm still here," I groaned, "but I don't want your food."

The food they served in the cafeteria was bad enough but the food they brought me in the hole was barely even food by the time it got to me.

"You have to eat dear," she sang out in a false sweet voice. "Dr. Matthews wants you to be big and strong."

"When is he going to let me out of here?"

"He'll let you out when you're no longer a threat to yourself or others," she recited the same response she gave every day.

"I'm fine," I growled. "Leslie is gone." *Maybe for good this time.*

"Here's your lunch, sweetie." She pushed a tray through the bottom part of the door. "Eat up."

"I'm not going to eat that."

She didn't reply, she was already gone. Of course she was - everyone was gone. Dr. Matthews had betrayed me. When he came to me in the hospital, I had thought he was there to help. Instead, he threw me in the hole so I could be completely by myself.

Leslie was gone. I hadn't seen her since that terrible day in the showers. Whatever they had given me must have chased her off.

I had been waiting for the day she would be gone; I had thought it would make me whole and normal. In reality, all I felt was empty. Maybe I didn't know how to be a whole and normal person.

~

The plate in front of me was full. It had been a long while since I was expected to eat so much food. My stomach jolted nervously. The hand that held onto my spoon was shaking.

"I don't want to eat this," I whispered to nurse Kaydee. She was sitting next to me on the bench style seating. I knew the cafeteria was full so I kept my eyes on the table. What could be gained by meeting they're stares?

Dr. Matthews guessed the medicine was working enough to let me out of solitaire, but not enough to let anyone sit with me.

"Just eat," she hissed back. "We all do things we don't like. Do you think I like sitting here?"

I took a breath and let it out through my nose. Why were we always fighting over oatmeal? I grabbed the spoon tightly in my hand. "Is everyone staring at me?" I asked, aware how childish I sounded.

"Don't worry about them." she snapped. "Why on earth would you worry about them when you have so much to worry about yourself?"

Rolling my eyes, I plunged the spoon into the stiff oatmeal. If I knew anything about Nurse Kaydee, I knew she wouldn't let me leave until I ate. I knew as soon as I saw her back in my room when I first got out that she was going to be worse than ever. *You've lost so much weight.*

"Why aren't you eating?" She nudged me with her bony elbow.

"I am." I waved the spoon in her direction. It was a bad move though - the oatmeal had congealed into a lump and my hand was shaking too bad. The food went flying off the spoon and flipped onto the table.

"Watch what you're doing," she scolded. "Just hurry up and eat Mellie."

As I chewed unenthusiastically on my oatmeal, I scanned the room for any signs of Leslie. I hadn't seen her in the hole - not once. I was half afraid that being back out with everyone else would bring her out of hiding.

So far it hadn't.

~

"You seem nervous."

My eyes darted around the familiar office. "I'm not nervous," I muttered through partially opened lips. "Why would I be nervous?"

"Is Leslie here?"

I jumped at the sound of her name. "No."

"It's been weeks since you left solitaire," Dr. Matthews commented. "You haven't seen her at all, have you?"

I chewed at the skin all around my thumb. "No," I jerked my head back and forth. "Not once."

"How do you feel about that?" His pen hovered over the paper.

"I..." I tried to swallow past my dry throat. "I'm not really sure."

"I thought you didn't want Leslie around anymore."

"I don't."

"And she's become dangerous."

"She's always been dangerous."

"You could have died that day in the shower."

"Yeah," I breathed.

"This is a good thing," he urged. "It's a step in the right direction."

Why didn't I feel like it was a good thing though? Why did my chest feel so tight? I nodded mutely, it was expected of me.

"I'm sure it'll get easier to see that," I told him - still nodding. "In time." Wasn't that what he always told me - just give it some time.

Dr. Matthews' eyes narrowed as he scribbled in his notebook. "We will change your meds," he promised.

"No!"

"No?"

"You'll make her come back."

"Don't worry, Mellie."

But I had heard those words from him many times before and there was always something to worry about. "I'm fine," I told him, putting my thumb back to my lips. "I just need time."

~

My nostrils flared as I exhaled heavily. Fingers shaking, I took the card that Nadia was holding out to me.

"Just pay attention to the game," she commanded from the corner of her mouth.

"Yeah," I jerked my body so I was leaning into the table - to prove how much I was paying attention. "I am."

"Your turn," Janice announced.

"Hurry up," Carrie clicked her tongue impatiently.

I quickly scanned my cards for a matching pair. Finding none, I discarded just as fast. "There," I panted.

"You're so weird," Carrie snarled, taking her own card.

On their own accord, my eyes drifted to the window seat. Leslie stared back at me, not smiling.

The game seem to be moving in slow motion. I wanted to be back in my room, just in case Leslie tried to do anything crazy. But Dr. Matthews insisted I sit out in the day room. Of course, he couldn't see Leslie or the way she stared at me. If he could, he wouldn't want me to be around anyone else - - not ever.

My heart started and faltered. I was going to be locked away forever. Leslie was never going to let me leave.

"Your turn," Carrie smacked her hand on the top of the table, making me jump.

"You shouldn't worry about her," Janice drawled out slowly.

"Carrie?" My top lip snarled up. "I'm not."

"Leslie."

My eyes widened. "How do you...?"

"Don't worry about any of them," Nadia grunted, handing me another card. "Dr. Matthews will figure out what meds work - that's his job."

Nadia wasn't like the rest of us, I realized as I watched her. She wasn't crazy. Something terrible had happened to her but it didn't break her. She wasn't like us.

"I know," I nodded. I put my last two cards on the table. "I win."

"That is such bullshit," Carrie screeched. "I only needed three more."

Without a word, Janice scooped up the cards and began to shuffle. "I'm not playing again *Janice*," Carrie continued in her high-pitched voice. "I don't want to play with crazy Mellie."

"You're just mad that you lost," Nadia fired back. She patted my hand, as if I needed comforting.

By the window, Leslie's eyes narrowed.

~

My eyes popped open. There was something terribly wrong. The room was dark but I could hear Leslie breathing heavily.

"What are you doing?" I scrambled to get myself up right on the bed.

"I'm doing this so we can stay together."

"Doing what?"

There was a sharp sting along my one arm. "This is the only way," she gasped. "I can't lose you."

"Leslie, stop it!"

She made another cut into my arm. Even though I couldn't see it, I could feel the blood dripping down. Leslie was trying to kill me again.

"Stop!"

The light flared to life. "What in the hell is going on in here?" A nurse stood in the doorway, her mouth hanging open.

~

"Where did you get the scissors?" Dr. Matthews asked again.

"I don't know." I pulled my bandaged arms closer to my chest. "I just woke up and she had them."

Dr. Matthews tapped his fingers against his desk. "You're lucky you didn't need any stitches."

"You keep saying I'm lucky..." My voice broke. "... But I don't feel lucky."

"If you want to be free of Leslie, you have to start fighting her."

"What?" I raised my head to look up at him. Where was his speech about everything being okay and we would find the right medications?

With a heavy sigh, he put his notebook on the desk and leaned towards me. "There's no magic pill to make everything perfect."

"I don't want to be perfect," I sobbed, "I just want to be normal."

"I believe with the medication you're on, you will be able to live a mostly normal life."

"Mostly." I held up my arms.

"You might always have Leslie with you..."

My eyes slid closed.

"... She's a part of you."

I really didn't want to hear any more. I always knew this day would come - the day Dr. Matthews told me I couldn't be fixed.

"There's so many people in this world living with their own versions of Leslie," he said quietly. "They just learn to cope with it; learn to coexist."

"How?"

"You have to be the one in charge."

"What if I can't?" Tears streamed freely down my face.

"You are strong enough. Do you believe that?"

"I..."

"Do you trust me?"

"Yes."

"Then trust me when I tell you that you are. I can see you more clearly than you see yourself." He moved his chair halfway across the room. "You let Leslie know who's boss," he half smiled, "then you can learn to cope too."

"Will I be normal?"

Dr. Matthews sighed. "I can't promise you'll be normal, but I *can* promise that if you can get this under control, I'll get you into those flower classes."

Hope flared to life in my broken heart.

~

Like a vulture, Leslie circled the table. She was nervous and angry - not a good combination. "I told you already," she seethed through her clenched teeth, "I don't want you to play cards with them."

"I don't care." I picked a card from the middle pile.

"Don't care about what?" Carrie howled.

"You," I shot back at her.

"That's good," she laughed loudly, "I don't like girls."

Rolling my eyes, I discarded.

"Not the way you do." Carrie picked up her card.

"I know what you're trying to do." Leslie dropped in front of me so her face was inches from mine.

"I'm trying to play cards," I swatted her away.

"You're trying to ignore me."

I moved in my seat to see around her. Dr. Matthews told me that my fear gave Leslie power. Not anymore.

Leslie swung her arm across the table and sent all the cards into Carrie's lap. "Mellie," Carrie screamed angrily. "You did that because I was winning."

In a flash, I was on my feet and glaring at Leslie. "I told you to leave me alone," I growled.

"No." She crossed her arms over her chest.

I'd had enough though. Surprising even myself, I lunged forward and pulled her arms apart. "Yes," I shouted back.

Her eyes widened. "Who do you think you are?" But I saw the fear flash in her familiar eyes.

"Leave. Me. Alone." I shoved her backwards. "Do you need me to say it again?"

Lips pulled back in a snarl, Leslie sprung forward to attack me. I was ready though. I met her head on and...

... She fell to the ground.

"Parker," nurse Kaydee bustled into the day room. "What is going on in here?" She glanced down to the cards all over the floor. "Back to your room," she barked out. "You know there's no fighting allowed in here."

"I won," I half whispered - amazed.

"Considering you were fighting thin air," she rolled her eyes, "congratulations."

Carrie's laughter turned to a snort. "Big bad Mellie," she squealed.

"Let's go," nurse Kaydee sighed, exasperated. But she didn't grip my arm very tight as she led me back to my room and as she shut the door, her eye dropped down into a quick wink.

~

Three years later

"Over here," I half stood in my seat so I could wave Dr. Matthews over.

"Mellie," he smiled wide as he took the seat across for me. "It's good to see you."

"You too," I gushed. "Thanks for meeting me here today."

"Of course." He glanced around the small coffee shop. "This is a nice place."

"This is my favorite place." I could barely keep the grin on my face from exploding. It was so nice to see Dr. Matthews outside of his small office building. "I ordered your favorite for you," I explained as a waitress came over with a white mug of coffee.

He leaned forward to inhale the scent coming from the top. "This isn't too far from your shop, is it?"

"Two stores over," I jerked my thumb towards the door. "And the bus stop is right out front."

One ten minute ride would take me straight to Tabby's boarding house. It was a nice place they had found for me to live, *just while I was getting my bearings.* I knew it was just so they could keep an eye on me but I didn't care.

"How's the flower shop going?" He took a small sip of coffee. Even though I saw Dr. Matthews every single week, he still always wanted to know the same things.

"Good," I nodded happily. "Daddy's pleased. He said he spent a mint on it so I better not go bankrupt," I grinned wide.

"And Nadia?"

"She got a new boyfriend," I sighed. "They're visiting his family in Florida for a few weeks."

"I thought she was helping out at the shop."

"Not anymore."

"Is it still just you and Mrs. Lin?"

"Remember, I told you we were going to hire a new girl."

Dr. Matthews nodded. "That's right. Mrs. Lin's son had a new baby."

"Yeah, so she only wants to do a few days a week in the shop."

"What's the new girl's name?"

"Kenzie."

"This coffee is good."

"I knew you'd like it. Do you want to go see the shop?"

"Absolutely."

"Good," my smile grew.

"Will you be back in the office next week?"

"Yep, I wouldn't miss our weekly dates for anything!"

"Except for today," he winked.

I laughed loudly. "I have to meet my mom. You know how much she hates for me to be late."

"How are the wedding plans going?"

"Good," I rolled my eyes. "Her new husband is so rich - I don't blame her for marrying him."

Dr. Matthews laughter boomed out over the table. It was a nice sound. "Ready?"

"Yep." I stood up to follow him out the door.

As we passed, my eyes strayed to the table in the corner. Leslie sat there alone, with her folded hands resting on the table. She smiled when our eyes locked and gave a tiny nod.

It didn't worry me that I could still see Leslie. Dr. Matthew said I probably always would. As he said - mental illness wasn't something that just went away, we just had to learn to cope.

Leslie was letting me live in my own small corner of the world and I was content. Really - that's all I wanted. It was enough.

Threading my arm through doctor Mathews' arm, we made our way down the busy sidewalk. My face was stretched in a wide smile that refused to leave.

"You've done well, Mellie," he said in that quiet way of his. "Very well."

The End

About the Author

Amy Richie has lived in a small town her entire life. She lives with her three kids and their cats, George and Ellie. She began writing in high school but never took it seriously until a few years ago. She enjoys writing because it takes her out of her everyday life and gives life to the people in her head. "When I was little I wanted to be a mermaid, then when I was in high school I wanted to be a vampire; now as an adult I'm a writer, which is better because now I get to be both."

Read more at amyrichie.weebly.com.